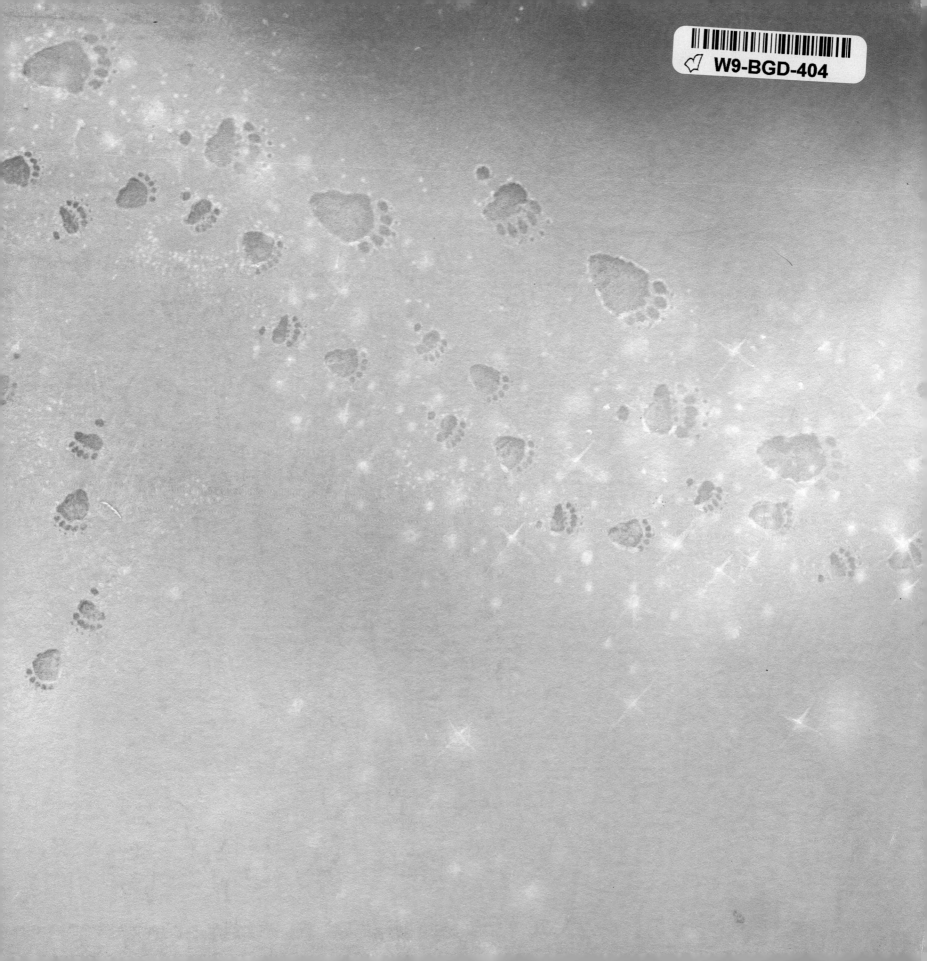

To David Brian Goodrich, whose beautiful mama will patiently tell him the whys of the world.
Welcome to Earth, little one.—K. W.

For James and Lucia
Love, Daddy—S. M.

MARGARET K. McELDERRY BOOKS • An imprint of Simon & Schuster Children's Publishing Division • 1230 Avenue of the Americas, New York, New York 10020 • Text copyright © 2011 by Karma Wilson • Illustrations copyright © 2011 by Simon Mendez • All rights reserved, including the right of reproduction in whole or in part in any form. • Margaret K. McElderry Books is a trademark of Simon & Schuster, Inc. • For information about special discounts for bulk purchases, please contact Simon & Schuster Special Sales at 1-866-506-1949 or business@simonandschuster.com. • The Simon & Schuster Speakers Bureau can bring authors to your live event. For more information or to book an event, contact the Simon & Schuster Speakers Bureau at 1-866-248-3049 or visit our website at www.simonspeakers.com. • Book edited by Emma D. Dryden • Book designed by Debra Sfetsios • The text for this book is set in Fink. • The illustrations for this book are rendered in mixed media. • Manufactured in China • 0111 SCP • 10 9 8 7 6 5 4 3 2 1 • Library of Congress Cataloging-in-Publication Data • Wilson, Karma. • Mama, why? / Karma Wilson ; illustrations by Simon Mendez—1st ed. • p. cm. • Summary: A sleepy polar bear cub asks its mother questions about the night sky as he gets ready to go to sleep. • ISBN 978-1-4169-4205-4 (hardcover) • [1. Stories in rhyme. 2. Sky—Fiction. 3. Night—Fiction. 4. Bedtime—Fiction. 5. Mother and child—Fiction. 6. Polar bear—Fiction. 7. Bears—Fiction.] I. Mendez, Simon, ill. II. Title. • PZ8.3.W6976Man 2011 • [E]—dc22 • 2009032205

FIRST EDITION

Mama, Why?

by **Karma Wilson**

illustrations by **simon mendez**

MARGARET K. MCELDERRY BOOKS

New York London Toronto Sydney

When the moon sails high in the arctic sky,

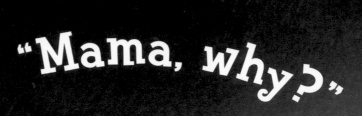

Polar Cub asks,

"Mama, why?"

Mama says,

"Moon floats up there
to say good night to polar bears.

"He glides above to shine sweet dreams

and sends them down on silver beams.

"And while you doze in soft moonlight,

you dream sweet dreams

from the moon so bright.

Dreams for you
from Moon in
the sky."

And Polar Cub asks,

"Mama, why?"

"Moon is friends with

the stars that glow,

and the stars tell Moon

the tales they know.

"They tell him of princes,

pirates, and queens,

of palaces,

Kingdoms,

and magical scenes.

"Such wondrous stories

the moon must share.

He turns them to dreams

for polar bears.

"Stories for you from the stars so high."

And Polar Cub asks,

"Mama, why?"

"Well," says Mama, "during the day

the stars leave the sky and wander away.

"They travel to lands both near and far–

the places they go, those curious stars!

"And while they travel, they see such sights.

They share them with Moon as they twinkle at night.

But come every day,

the stars say good-bye."

And Polar Cub asks,

"Mama, why?"

"Well, stars don't sleep like you or me.

Instead they travel the galaxy.

They sometimes sprinkle dust as they go—

and stardust,

my dear, is what

we call snow.

"So now, little one, let's rest our heads,

and dream moonbeams in a stardust bed.

I'll dream of my dearest

the whole night through."

And Polar Cub asks,

"Mama, who?"

Mama whispers softly,

"You."

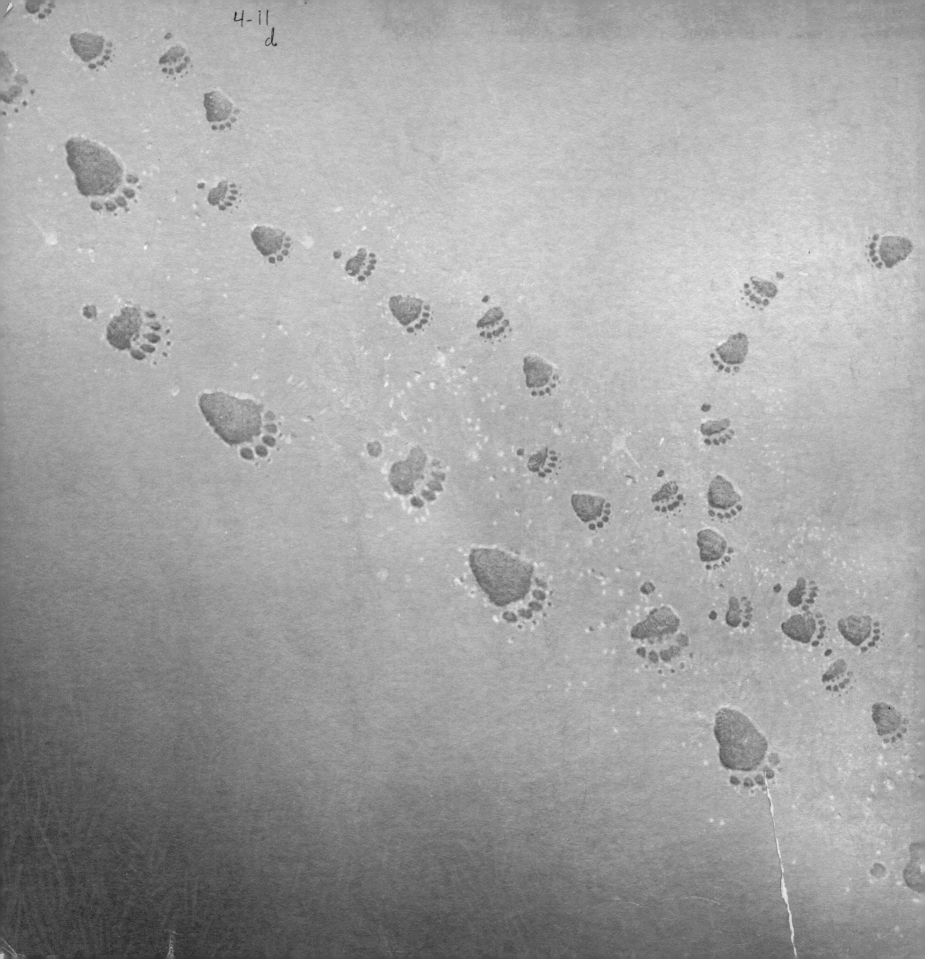